THE TREK

Ann Jonas

MULBERRY BOOKS • New York

For Susan,
and of course,
Don, Nina + Amy

Library of Congress
Cataloging in Publication Data
Jonas, Ann.   The trek.
Summary: A child describes
her trip through a jungle and
across a desert—right
on the way to school.
1. Children's stories, American.
[1. Jungles—Fiction.
2. Deserts—Fiction.
3. Imagination—Fiction]   I. Title.
PZ7.J664Tr 1985   [E]   84-25962
 ISBN 0-688-08742-6

My mother
doesn't walk me
to school anymore.

But she doesn't know
we live on the edge
of a jungle.

She doesn't even see
what's right outside our door!

There are creatures everywhere.
But they can't hide from me.

Some of my animals are dangerous
and it's only my amazing skill
that saves me day after day.

Look at that!
The waterhole is really
crowded today.

What will they do when this herd
goes down to drink?

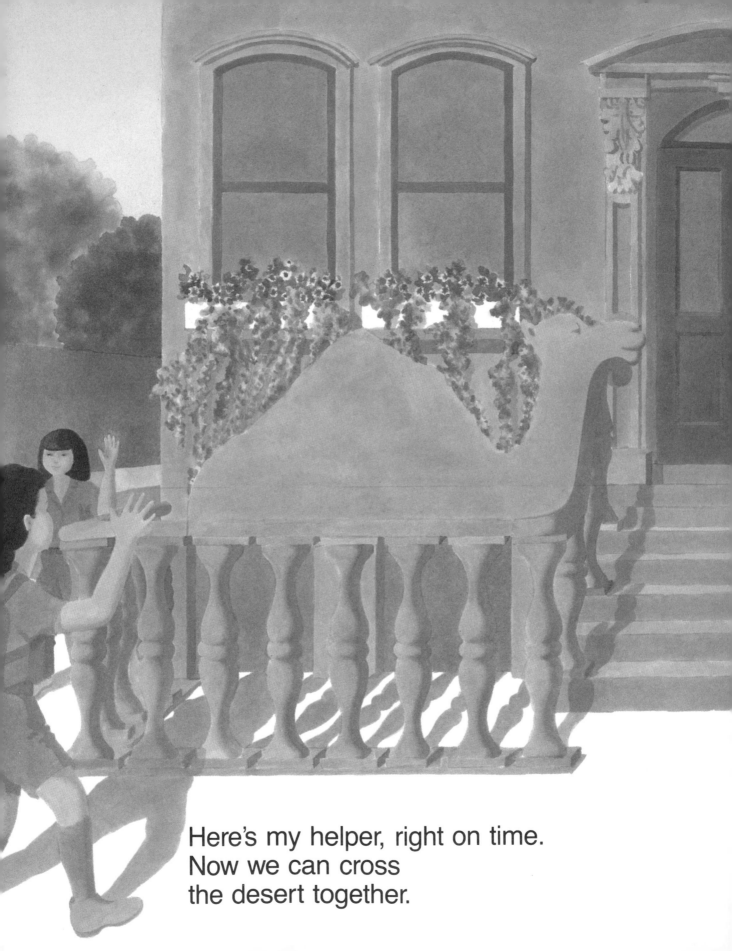

Here's my helper, right on time.
Now we can cross
the desert together.

Those animals won't see us
if we stay behind the sand dunes.
Be very quiet.

That woman doesn't know
about the animals.
If she did, she'd be scared.

We missed the boat!
Now we'll have to swim
across the river.

Be careful! This jungle is full of animals.

The trading post at last!
No time to stop!

We're almost there, only the mountain to climb.

We made it!

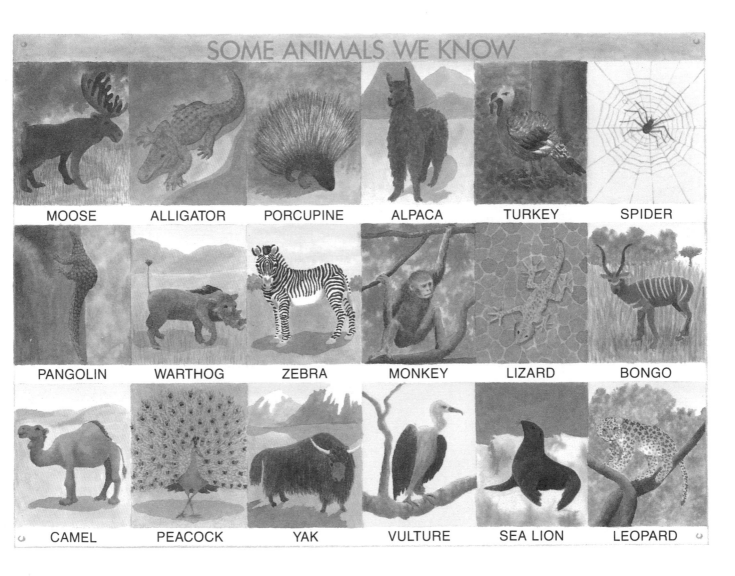

SOME ANIMALS WE KNOW

MOOSE   ALLIGATOR   PORCUPINE   ALPACA   TURKEY   SPIDER

PANGOLIN   WARTHOG   ZEBRA   MONKEY   LIZARD   BONGO

CAMEL   PEACOCK   YAK   VULTURE   SEA LION   LEOPARD

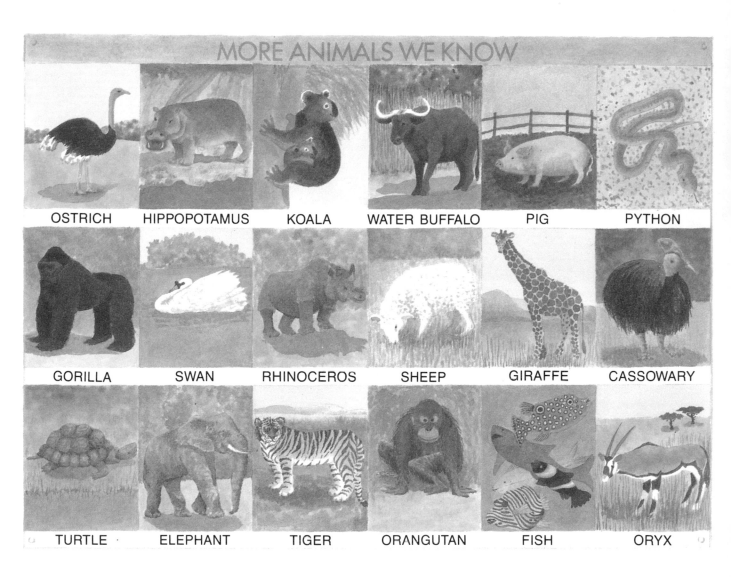

MORE ANIMALS WE KNOW

OSTRICH HIPPOPOTAMUS KOALA WATER BUFFALO PIG PYTHON

GORILLA SWAN RHINOCEROS SHEEP GIRAFFE CASSOWARY

TURTLE ELEPHANT TIGER ORANGUTAN FISH ORYX